GOSCINNY AND UDERZO
PRESENT
AN ASTERIX ADVENTURE

Asterix
OPERATION GETAFIX

THE BOOK OF THE FILM

TRANSLATED BY ANTHEA BELL AND DEREK HOCKRIDGE

HODDER AND STOUGHTON
LONDON   SYDNEY   AUCKLAND   TORONTO

This book is based on the film ASTERIX AND THE BIG
FIGHT, produced by Yannik Piel for Gaumont, Gaumont
Production and Extrafilm Produktion. The script was written
by Yannik Voight from the books, ASTERIX AND THE
SOOTHSAYER and ASTERIX AND THE BIG FIGHT,
both published by Hodder Dargaud. The film was made by
Philippe Grimond, Keith Ingham, Michel Guérin, Thierry
Fournier, Michael Gabriel, Miguel Angel Gil and Michel
Pisson. This book was designed by Patrick Couratin and
Frederick Mei. Photography by Serge Masi.

British Library Cataloguing in Publication Data

Goscinny, *1926–1977*
Operation Getafix: Goscinny and Uderzo present an Asterix adventure.
I. Title   II. Uderzo   III. Coup du menhir. *English*
741.5944

ISBN 0-340-52945-8

First published in Great Britain 1990

Published by Hodder and Stoughton Children's Books,
a division of Hodder and Stoughton Ltd,
Mill Road, Dunton Green, Sevenoaks, Kent TN13 2YA

Printed in Belgium by Proost International Book Production

The year is 50 BC. Gaul is entirely occupied by the Romans. Well, not entirely... One small village of indomitable Gauls still holds out against the invaders. And life is not easy for the Roman legionaries who garrison the fortified camps of Totorum, Aquarium, Laudanum and Compendium...

By Toutatis, that had been a useful little stroll! Obelix and I were on our way back from the forest, each of us with a boar slung over his shoulders. We love hunting wild boar. We like hunting Romans next best. Unlike the wild boar, however, the Roman legionary is not a solitary animal. Roman soldiers always go about in groups. Funny habit, that. They claim the idea is to keep the *Pax Romana.*

We saw our druid Getafix coming. He was out for a breath of fresh air himself, this nice fine day.

'Well, boys, any news?' Getafix asked us.

'No. Good hunting, same as usual.'

'But I had Dogmatix to help me. He's a great boarhound!' said Obelix, fondly.

'Oh yes,' I added. 'I was forgetting. We bumped into a Roman patrol.'

'These Romans are crazy,' Obelix commented.

Getafix went quietly on his way to the forest clearing, a place he knows well. It's where he picks the ingredients he needs for his secret recipe. The secret recipe for the magic potion. The magic potion which has made us famous. (And not just in occupied Gaul either!)

Busy gathering herbs, our druid didn't notice anything odd. Not the spinney lurching about like a ship at sea, not the helmets decorating the branches, nor the feet shifting restlessly under the leaves. Those were really very peculiar bushes. Bushes giving a lively imitation of camouflaged Roman soldiers from the fortified camp of Compendium, pretending to be part of the Armorican landscape.

Those Romans get everywhere!

Sickle raised, Getafix was about to gather a rather strange plant. A plant resembling a Roman toe. The legionary on the other end of it let out a yell. Instantly, and as one bush, the spinney flung itself on the druid, gagged him, and started dragging him off to the Roman camp. Things were moving too fast for poor Getafix. He only had time to utter a faint moan.

Obelix and I had been watching this unusual rural scene, transfixed with horror. But now I rushed to Getafix's aid, shouting, 'Our druid! The Romans!'

'Don't worry, I'll get rid of them for you,' said Obelix, grabbing a good-sized menhir and aiming at the Roman bushes, who immediately took to their roots and ran for it.

BOOOM! The menhir landed right on top of Getafix. I suppose it was a good throw, but I was furious. Really furious.

'Bravo, Obelix! Oh, well done!' I said.

'Er . . . well,' muttered that great oaf Obelix, slightly miffed, 'well, I did get rid of them, didn't I?'

He picked up the menhir and released our flattened druid.

'Now what do we do?' I asked.

'We could blow him up again!' suggested Obelix, brightly.

Frantic with anxiety, we carried Getafix back to the village square and put him down under a tree. Hearing the news, all the villagers came running up in alarm. But luckily our druid is tough.

'Look, he's coming back to his senses,' I said. 'How are you feeling, Getafix?'

'Very well, thank you,' said the druid, politely. 'And who might you be, my dear sir?'

'I'm Asterix!' I cried. 'You know me . . . Asterix!'

'Pleased to meet you,' said the druid, rising to his feet. He looked at us all, and then burst out laughing. 'Ho, ho, ho, ho! Oh, what a funny lot you are!'

Greatly relieved, Obelix rushed over to him. 'I'm so glad you're all right. I always knew a little menhir like that couldn't do worse than tickle him . . .'

'Ho, ho, ho, ho! You really ARE funny, fatty! Ho, ho, ho, ho!' chuckled the druid.

Obelix did not appreciate the druid's sense of humour. On the other hand, it was the perfect opportunity for our bard Cacofonix, who struck up a song. To the amazement of all and sundry, Getafix applauded. He even asked for an encore!

HE'S GONE MAD! GETAFIX HAS GONE MAD!

'He . . . he's gone crazy!' I cried. 'OUR DRUID GETAFIX HAS GONE CRAZY!'

Well, he had to be crazy to enjoy the bard's singing!!! Everyone was looking dazed.

'He's lost his memory!'

Who could tell how Getafix's mind was working now? Maybe he saw the big fat man leaning over him float up in the air, turn square, come down to earth again and strut like a rooster. Or maybe he was looking at our songbird Cacofonix warbling away and thinking: What talent! What a sense of rhythm! What a magnificent performance, unique in the musical history of Armorica!

'He's got menhir-stroke! He's got menhir-stroke!' The words were taken up by a chorus of village women dipping and swaying, carried away by the music.

It never rains but it pours! Large black clouds were gathering over the village. Even the elements were ganging up on us! The wind rose. There was a flash of lightning, followed by a dull rumble, and then Taranis the thunder-god let fly. Rain swept the village, the trees bent under the force of the wind, while the huts did their best to stand up to it. Why such a storm? What was that strange, menacing shadow on the wet ground, looming in the distance, coming closer? Ancient, ancestral fear crept into the minds of all the Gaulish villagers — a fear which has haunted us from generation to generation. Was the sky about to fall on our heads? Normally Getafix would protect us, but how could he help us now?

Ancestral or not, fear is infectious. Vitalstatistix's house was soon sheltering the whole village. Everyone was there, young and old, women and children, trembling with terror as they pressed close. The fishmonger tried to defy Fate by shaking a fish at the sky. Vitalstatistix himself was badly shaken by the storm. He looked really worried. Obelix and I tried to lighten the atmosphere, but it was a sheer waste of time: the storm had stolen the show. Even the bard with his singing couldn't compete!

CRAAAASH! Taranis was going great guns now. That tremendous crash of thunder was followed by total silence. And then we heard three knocks. A dazzling light flashed in the open doorway. There stood a vast and terrifying shape, half man, half beast. Where did it come from? From what depths had it risen? How had it got here? Nobody moved. All the villagers were petrified.

'Well, Chief Vitalstatistix, aren't you going to ask our visitor in?' I suggested.

Trembling, Vitalstatistix stepped forward. 'Who are you, traveller?' he asked.

'My name,' said the stranger, 'is Prolix. I **knew** the storm was going to break, so I hurried to your home, where I **knew** I could count on your hospitality.'

'How – however did you know all that?' asked Vitalstatistix.

'Because I AM A SOOTHSAYER!' the visitor announced.

'A SOOTHSAYER!?!' exclaimed the villagers, in chorus.

Crash! So it wasn't the sky falling on our heads after all, just a soothsayer dropping in on us – and falling foul of me! I can't stand his sort! I hate that wild, woolly, wandering-soothsayer look. By all the gods of ancient Gaul, I just don't trust those charlatans! Exploiting the people, thriving on credulity and fear. Personally, I could foretell without the shadow of a doubt that this one meant trouble. And Getafix was still under the influence of the menhir!

'Someone in this room,' remarked the soothsayer, nastily, 'is sceptical, and Taranis the thunder-god doesn't like sceptics.'

Taranis was certainly still deafening us in his frenzied rage. Outside, the sky grew dark, illuminated only by flashes of lightning. But nothing, absolutely nothing, shook my belief that Toutatis, the god of our own village, would protect us. We'd had storms before. We'd have storms again. So why panic?

We offered the soothsayer refreshments. Obelix grabbed the only roast boar in the house, leaving our visitor a bowl of milk. Obelix has always had his own ideas about sharing, particularly when it comes to food.

Impedimenta, the chief's wife, who was scared of the thunderstorm, couldn't help asking the soothsayer the old, old question. 'Is the sky about to fall on our heads, or isn't it?'

The soothsayer said he would need to read the entrails of an animal to find out. And the look in his eyes as he stared at Dogmatix showed all too clearly what he was thinking. The little dog jumped into Obelix's arms, yelping.

'**The first person to touch Dogmatix gets a biff up the hooter!**' said Obelix, furiously.

'Watch out, soothsayer!' I added. 'Obelix's predictions often come true!'

Ever ready to cooperate, particularly when he sees a chance of getting rid of surplus stock, Unhygienix the fishmonger offered a fish well past its sell-by date. The soothsayer buried himself in reading its entrails.

'By Borvo, god of springs . . . and by Damona the heifer . . . and no matter what any sceptics may think – I see that the sky will not fall on your heads, and that when the storm is over the weather will improve.'

'Oh, what a relief!' cried Impedimenta. And she wasn't the only one! All the ladies were happy now, and full of admiration for the soothsayer's talents.

'I also see that there's going to be a fight,' he added.

This was too much! Just too much! Couldn't they tell that the soothsayer was merely stringing platitudes together, the way you might string beads? I exploded!

'If Getafix was here he'd tell you not to believe this imposter! This is ridiculous!'

'It is dangerous to deny the existence of the gods,' intoned the druid. His remarks were beginning to get on my nerves.

'But, Asterix, the fish has spoken!' protested the infatuated Impedimenta.

A fish! Could anything smelling like that still be called a fish?

For a change the soothsayer agreed with me. 'The news certainly was a bit stale,' he said.

The only accurate prediction you could make about Unhygienix's fish was that anyone who ate it would be ill! The blacksmith agreed with me there. 'Now it's been read, you ought to close it up and put it back on the slab,' he told Unhygienix.

I've noticed before that the fishmonger is very touchy about the freshness of his stock. **POW!** Seizing the fish like a club, he brought it down on the blacksmith's head. Next moment the fight was raging . . . crockery flying through the air, blows raining down. Had everyone else gone mad as well as the druid? This was no time for us to enjoy ourselves!

The soothsayer watched the deplorable scene with satisfaction. Taking advantage of the general confusion, he slipped over to the doorway. As he opened the door, light flooded into the room.

'Just as I predicted, now the storm is over, the weather has improved!' he announced. 'I'm leaving you now. Other villages need my skills.'

'Oh, don't go, soothsayer!' wailed Impedimenta.

Good riddance, if you ask me!

But to return to our troubles, by which I mean Getafix, he was still suffering from the effects of that menhir. At his bedside, Vitalstatistix asked, 'How are we going to cure him, Asterix? Surely there must be some way?'

'To think how easily Getafix could have made potions to cure himself,' I said . . . and then I realised! 'The potion! The magic potion!'

But Getafix was still wool-gathering, daft as a brush and perfectly happy. He didn't seem to understand. 'Magic potion?' he asked us innocently. 'What magic potion? And who's this Getafix you keep going on about?'

'This is a very serious situation,' muttered Chief Vitalstatistix, shaking his head. 'Suppose the Romans find out our druid is ill . . .'

There was no time to lose! Without potion, we were vulnerable. Vitalstatistix and I lit a fire under the cauldron. Obelix collected all the ingredients he could find.

'What do you want me to do?' asked Getafix. He obviously still didn't understand what was going on.

'Well – er – you put the ingredients in the cauldron,' I said.

At least that bit of it amused him no end. In it all went – a pinch of saffron, a carrot, a bunch of leeks, a cabbage, an armful of I don't know what, a small glass of some mysterious brown liquid . . .

With all this mixture in it, the cauldron was bubbling nicely. Cheerful as ever, but a bit apprehensive now, Getafix took fright. He flung himself into Obelix's arms, like a child. At least my friend's solid figure seemed to reassure him this time. But Vitalstatistix and I were still worried.

'Looks as though he remembers the formula,' Vitalstatistix whispered.

Getafix went back to his mixture. It was going BLOP, BLOP, BLOP! He carried on with the good work, turning to ask me, 'Do I put this in too?'

BOOOM! The cauldron exploded, shot up into the air, and disappeared.

Maybe he'd just got the quantities wrong? Getafix wasn't letting a little thing like an explosion bother him. 'Teeheehee! Let's start again!' he said.

Obelix went to find another cauldron. We just had to get it right. Or rather, Getafix had to get it right. He alone knew the secret of the magic potion on which our fate depended. As everyone knows by now, Obelix fell into it when he was a baby, and it had a permanent effect on him. But what about the rest of us, who hadn't been so lucky? What was to become of us?

BOOM! Another cauldron exploded, taking off like a menhir when thrown by Obelix.

Out in the clearing, a Roman patrol was advancing cautiously, shields at the ready. They all knew what they risked on such dangerous ground. They had vivid memories of their last little stroll in the forest. In fact, those memories were as firmly fixed in their heads as a menhir in the ground ... except that menhirs were airborne today. So they kept their eyes and ears open. Legionary Infirmofpurpus, leading the patrol, couldn't place the funny metallic whistling sound somewhere above the treetops. He hesitated, and stopped for a moment to find out what was going on.

A flying cauldron landed on his helmet. He couldn't even squeak before his arms were swallowed up too. In fact he was swallowed up entirely. It was a large and splendid cauldron, meant for fish soup, and it fitted him beautifully, leaving nothing of him showing but his sandalled feet and his hands.

You have to admit it was an intriguing sight. In his madness, Getafix had taken perfect aim. Thus adorned, the patrol went back to camp empty-handed. The legionaries made their report, explaining what had happened to the centurion, who was in his bath.

'They're making horrible noises in that village ...'

'And firing cauldrons great distances ...'

'Winkle that idiot out of there,' was the martial reply of the centurion, as he examined all that showed of Infirmofpurpus and sniffed the fishy cauldron. 'And tell him he's volunteered to go and spy on the Gauls.'

Infirmofpurpus was not enthusiastic about this idea. On due reflection, he felt greatly attached to his cauldron. Why leave it, when they were an inseparable couple? His companions, however, did not share this point of view, particularly as they were well aware that if Infirmofpurpus didn't carry out his mission, someone else would have to volunteer. Placed over the fire, the Roman felt his cheeks begin to burn ...

The soothsayer had been sorry to leave the village. He was also leaving a lot of potential customers behind. He knew that hope, being all in the mind, is an ever-expanding market, and well worth a few frauds. His was a simple recipe: a spot of illusion, a suggestion of mystery, just enough to keep his public in suspense. With a stock in trade ranging from riddles to sheer nonsense, you can rake in the sestertii. It was as good a way as any of providing for his old age without going to unnecessary trouble. Of course, the drawback was that now and then soothsayers come across sceptics like Obelix and me. Well, you can't foresee everything! So this particular soothsayer had decided it would be better to clear off. Alone in the forest, he was on his way towards some other destiny. And when it was time to stop for refreshments, he found only a crust of bread in his bag. Contrary to expectations, the omens for the future did not look too good.

However, Impedimenta still wanted more conversation with the soothsayer to soothe her anxiety. She longed to know if she would ever make it to the high society of Lutetia, and she wasn't going to miss this once-in-a-lifetime chance of finding out. Hearing her approach, the soothsayer rose and went on his way. Like the ham actor he was, he assumed an inscrutable expression.

'Soothsayer!' called Impedimenta. 'Hey, wait a minute, soothsayer!

BOOOOM! Somewhere in the distance, a cauldron exploded. What a gift for the soothsayer!

'You see, the gods are still angry!' he said. 'I warned you of the dangers of showing disrespect to a soothsayer!'

'Don't leave, soothsayer. I wanted to consult you about my future!'

'No, no, no! There are sceptics in your village,' said the soothsayer. 'That little man with the yellow moustache, and the great fat monster who won't let anyone read his dog!'

Obelix and I figured large in the following conversation. Impedimenta was tactful. She wanted to keep her soothsayer where she could talk to him, but she realised there are limits! However, she thought of a solution . . . why shouldn't he camp there in the clearing? She promised to bring him things to eat.

'Oh no, we soothsayers lead a life of meditation!' said Prolix loftily. 'Just bring me something to read: boars, ducks, chickens, beer . . .'

'Can you read beer too?'

'If it's well brewed it becomes very legible,' said the soothsayer.

And there in the dark wood – but beginning to feel he was out of the wood now – he painted Impedimenta a picture of her dazzling future. She went home delighted. On the way, she met Geriatrix's wife, and couldn't help telling her the secret. Charming young Mrs Geriatrix loved sharing things. Especially secrets. With characteristic generosity, she went from house to house with this one, making the local temperature rise considerably.

All was calm. After a number of explosive experiments, Getafix had perfected a new recipe. One which didn't explode. Was it THE potion? I suggested we could find out by using a taster. Preferably a Roman. After all, the bushes were full of them. Out in the forest we met Impedimenta, who looked happy, but rather flustered to see us! Impedimenta was behaving oddly these days. Obelix suggested hunting a boar or so to take home, but without giving us the chance to say another word she invited us to dinner with her and Vitalstatistix. To be honest, this was not the moment for dinner-parties!

'Are you turning down an invitation from your chief's wife, Asterix?' she asked.

Shelving our mission for the time being, we found Chief Vitalstatistix in his hut, soaking his feet. We could hardly believe our ears when we heard Impedimenta address him in the following affectionate terms:

'I've brought some guests home, Piggywiggy!'

Piggywiggy! Had she really called him Piggywiggy? Obelix and I didn't dare look at each other. We could feel we were about to burst out laughing. We couldn't help it! Obelix cracked first.

'Oh, Pedimenta darling, you haven't called me Piggywiggy since we were first married!' said Vitalstatistix.

When it comes to a good joke, my resistance threshold is low, and I fell about laughing myself. It's a well-known fact that chiefs don't like ridicule (especially when it's directed at them). Vitalstatistix was no exception.

'What's the matter with you two?' he snapped. And he added, turning to his wife, 'May I ask why you saw fit to invite these two clowns to dinner?'

'Why, because they're the best warriors in the village, Piggywiggy! The druid's ill, and the Romans could attack the village at any time.'

'The Romans are lying low at the moment,' Vitalstatistix pointed out.

'Yes, but you never know with them, and we're out of magic potion. Asterix and Obelix shouldn't leave the village to go into the forest just now, Piggywiggy.'

Gasping for breath, I tried to say something useful. 'Listen, Chief Piggyw . . .'

But the rest of it was drowned out by Obelix's roars of laughter, which drew down the wrath of our chief on his head.

'Oh, so you think it's funny, do you? Well, you can just stay in the village and guard our druid, and that's an order!'

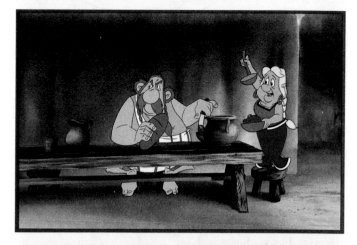

Out in the forest, things were unusually lively. Impedimenta was striding briskly along, with a basket crammed with food over her arm. She didn't notice anything odd. Not even the mobile tree-trunk with the owl doing gymnastics on it.

'O soothsayer, I've brought you something to read!' she announced. 'It's about my future in Lutetia.' Then her face fell. 'How silly of me! This goose is stuffed! It hasn't got any entrails!'

'Never mind,' the soothsayer reassured her. 'I get tired of reading tripe.'

Sitting at the edge of the crater created by Getafix's experiments, we were helplessly watching the druid's further fruitless attempts when Geriatrix passed by, bent double under the weight of an amphora. Where was he going? Even Unhygienix was taking his fish for a breath of fresh air!

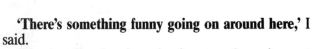

'**There's something funny going on around here,**' I said.

'They're all going into the forest and coming out happy, that's what's going on,' said Obelix. He was right, too. At this very moment, Chief Vitalstatistix came out of the forest, humming.

'Hey, chief!'

But he didn't see or hear us.

'What on earth *is* going on in that forest???' I wondered. Why did they all look so happy? They went into the forest with armfuls of stuff, and came out empty-handed, gazing into the wide blue yonder. What was the reason for this peculiar behaviour?

Dogmatix was the first to spot the tree with the owl on it. A tree in a forest is normal. An owl perched on a tree is normal too. But this particular tree was walking and talking, and then it hid itself, inefficiently, behind the village fence. Intent on our experiments, we hadn't noticed it before. However, Dogmatix's instincts told him there was something fishy about that tree.

WOOF! WOOF! The camouflaged legionary ran for it. Obelix caught Infirmofpurpus without any trouble at all and brought him back to our own cauldron, extricating him from his disguise.

'Look at this, Asterix! My first legionary disguised as a tree!'

'Don't hurt me!' begged the Roman.

'We're not going to hurt you,' I said. 'We're offering you a spot of soup, that's all.'

And I held out a ladle full of the stuff to Infirmofpurpus. He was idiot enough to swallow it meekly (they train their troops to total obedience in the Roman Army). By Toutatis, he was going green! Another ladle of the mixture, and he went blue! And now he was striped like Obelix's breeches! Getafix just went on adding more ingredients to his potion. The Roman turned into a lion. Then he grew a dragon's tail. The rhythm was speeding up. Ladle by ladle, we watched some very interesting transformations. Suddenly our taster swelled up . . . and up . . . to double, to three times, to four times his normal size. **HELP!**

None of these changes bothered our druid, absorbed as he was in his research. Yet another ladle full of potion, and the Roman was reduced in size, and reduced some more, and some more . . . and we hadn't even brought him to the boil!

Here Getafix delicately picked him up and dropped him in the soup. SPLOSH! If this went on much longer our experiments would tire poor Infirmofpurpus out.

Finally we got back to a faithful replica of the original legionary. Could this be the right recipe?

'How are you feeling, Roman?' I asked.

'Fine! In the pink,' he said, examining his skin, which was its proper colour again. 'Positively buoyant . . . **very buoyant! HELP! CATCH ME!'**

He was floating up in the air and flying away, to the delight of his friend the owl.

Meanwhile in the camp of Compendium, the centurion was sething with impatience. The sentry on duty at the gate was having a peaceful snooze. But not for long.

'Hey!'

Where did that voice come from? He rubbed his eyes. Looked around him. Nothing. No, it was up above! Good heavens! By Jupiter, there were some odd things going on in this fortified camp! Who was that, flying overhead? Why, it was the legionary who had volunteered to go spying, accompanied by an owl! Was this some cunning new kind of camouflage?

'Send me up an anchor, and none of your clever remarks!' yelled Infirmofpurpus.

Once Infirmofpurpus was attached to the end of a rope, the sentry towed him off to the centurion, who was in a bad temper. The sight of the legionary flying in the air didn't soothe him. Far from it.

'That's no way to appear before your commanding officer!' he snapped. 'Come down here at once!'

'I can't! I'm light as a feather!' wailed Infirmofpurpus.

'Feather-brained, more like. Bring him down!' the centurion ordered.

Infirmofpurpus sounded a bit strung up as he made his report, but he went through it in detail: about the druid, the cauldron, the soup . . . and the experiments in which he had been a guinea pig. He described them and their side-effects in great detail . . . he'd really taken to spying, and knew the ropes by now.

'Their druid is experimenting with new potions and having no end of fun,' he reported.

'Huh!' grunted the centurion. 'That was all we needed!'

Infirmofpurpus couldn't be allowed to spread his wings, though; he might yet come in useful. So the centurion ordered him to be fixed to a tent peg, which did not seem to please him particularly.

Infirmofpurpus, light as a feather, had flown back to camp to make his report. So now the whole Roman camp knew there were odd things going on in the village. The centurion did some hard thinking.

'What can they be planning?' he wondered.

He prudently decided to send a patrol to observe the invincible Gauls. Perhaps they weren't as invincible as all that any more! If cauldrons were going off bang, and the druid was losing his powers, then the village was at his mercy. Where Caesar had failed, HE might succeed!

'I shall conquer all Gaul!' the centurion told himself. He loved, admired, and envied Caesar . . . he dreamed of being a noble conqueror and going down in history himself. And now his moment had come.

'There are some very funny things going on around here . . . what exactly are they up to in that forest?' I asked. 'Obelix, you keep an eye on Getafix!'

And disobeying Vitalstatistix's orders, I set off. I came to a clearing, where a strange scene met my eyes. A soft featherbed was spread on the ground. Who was it for? Someone who ate a lot, certainly. As witness the remains of several meals, chicken carcasses, well picked boar bones . . . empty jugs, barrels of the best beer . . . By Toutatis, there was enough for a banquet here! Who could be indulging himself in good living like this?

'Anyone at home?' I called.

Then I saw Impedimenta, carrying a dish of steaming hot roast boar on a bed of appetizing vegetables. I don't know which of us was more surprised. Like the polite and chivalrous Gaul I am, I went to help her. Impedimenta didn't thank me, as you might have expected. She started shouting instead.

'**Where is he?**'

'Where is **who**?'

I couldn't make head or tail of this.

'**You've driven him away!**' she screeched, like a Fury. 'Didn't your chief tell you not to go into the forest?'

And turning on her heel, she set off for the village at a run. I couldn't leave her like that, especially as I still didn't know who it was I was supposed to have driven away. Impedimenta was shouting louder and louder, rousing the whole village.

'**This will bring great misfortune down on us!**' she wailed. '**The soothsayer warned me!**'

'**The soothsayer**'

I'd certainly seen him leave – but just where had he gone? I ran after Impedimenta, who was spreading panic as she ran through the village, shouting.

ASTERIX HAS DRIVEN THE SOOTHSAYER AWAY!

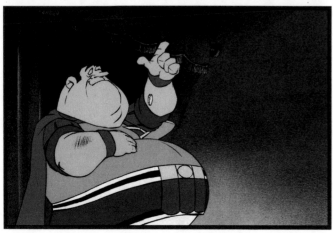

And if I'd known where that bird of ill omen was, I certainly would have driven him away. For once, the Romans had done a public service. They'd taken that wretched soothsayer off our hands. He'd been picked up by the Roman patrol. Incredible but true! The optio got back to camp.

'*Ave*, Centurion!' he reported. 'On proceeding on patrol for which you gave the orders to proceed with, we found this 'ere individual in a clearing, and after a caution he made a statement what we were not very satisfied with.'

The news didn't seem to please the centurion much.

'A Gaulish prisoner?' he bellowed. **'Are you out of your tiny minds?** You there,' he added, turning to the soothsayer, 'are you one of those savages still holding out against us?'

The soothsayer wasn't putting up any great show of defiance. 'Me? Oh no, I'm not one of those villagers! I don't hold out against anyone! Dear me, no. Look, my name's Prolix, and I'm travelling the country in search of a patrol. I'm a soothsayer.'

'A soothsayer ... hm. Are you really a genuine Gaulish soothsayer?' asked the centurion.

'Of course. For instance, I foretell that you'll be promoted. You will do great deeds.'

'Like conquering the indomitable Gauls?'

'Just what I was about to say myself.'

'Well, you're out of luck, soothsayer. We've got orders from Rome to arrest *all* Gaulish soothsayers.'

'No, no, I was only joking. I'm not a real soothsayer at all. I'm a fake.'

'But you just foretold that I'd be promoted!'

'Well, the fact is, I take advantage of people's credulity to make a living without working, see?'

However, the centurion was not convinced. He produced a coin. At the sight of the gold, the soothsayer's eyes widened like Roman shields. 'Heads or tails?' asked the centurion.

'Neither,' said the soothsayer, hands demurely folded.

The centurion tossed the coin. It turned, hesitated, started moving the opposite way, fell and came to a halt ... on its side.

'You win!' said the centurion. 'I knew he was a real soothsayer as soon as he said I'd get promotion.'

Was he a real soothsayer or wasn't he? The soothsayer got terribly involved in preposterous explanations. He described the Gauls as simple-minded, stupid folk, ready to believe anything he told them, and highly credulous. All of a sudden, the centurion got the idea for a really cunning piece of Roman strategy. If the Gauls would believe anything the soothsayer told them, then he must return to the village and persuade them to leave it. A brilliant notion!

On reaching the village gates, the soothsayer eyed the crowd assembled around our chief. Just as Vitalstatistix was telling me how dangerous it was to defy a soothsayer, Impedimenta, the first to spot him, screeched:

> ## LOOK!

'LOOK! THE SOOTHSAYER! THE SOOTH-SAYER IS BACK!'

Obviously there was no getting rid of the wretched man! Help! Something had to be done. I could feel that the villagers were still ready to believe anything he told them. This was terrible. They were all affected! What could I do? As I racked my brains, I was deaf to the soothsayer haranguing the crowd, terrifying my poor friends as he uttered words laden with menace. I'm sure the villagers thought it was all true.

'Yes, Gauls,' the soothsayer announced, 'I am back to tell you that misfortune has come upon you. Your village is CURSED by the gods. The very air you breathe will rise from the depths of hell. It will be foul, poisoned, and your faces will turn a ghastly hue ... **FLEE! FLEE, RASH PEOPLE! IT IS YOUR ONLY CHANCE OF SURVIVAL! DON'T SAY I DIDN'T WARN YOU!'**

Aware of his responsibilities, Vitalstatistix decided to respect the so-called will of the gods.

'We'll go and camp on the little island just off the coast,' he said.

This was ridiculous. I didn't agree. 'I'm staying,' I said.

Obelix nearly went. But at the last moment, thanks to Dogmatix, who had taken refuge in my arms, he decided not to embark. I was glad of that, but we had no time to lose.

'The Romans may attack at any moment. We'd better go and hide in the forest,' I said.

Getafix, Obelix and I were left alone, abandoned by all the others. The druid, who didn't seem to realise any of that, went on playing with his potions. There was a violent explosion. The cauldron spat fire like a volcano erupting. In alarm, I ran to help the old man.

'Stand back, Getafix!'

There was another and even bigger bang. And another. The flames were followed by suffocating smoke, pouring relentlessly up from the cauldron. It spread onwards and outwards, covering the country around us with thick vapour. What was happening to me? I couldn't breathe. I was choking. My legs had gone wobbly. I felt weak. All was dark, and I was falling.

But Obelix had seen the smoke overcome me. He called to me, made his way through the tide of smoke, and fished me out, unconscious. Carefully, he put my lifeless body down on a rock.

The scene that followed was to give more than one person the horrors. The soothsayer arrived in the village, accompanied by the centurion, who in turn was escorted by a troop of legionaries. All present and correct! The soothsayer with the Romans: that explained everything!

Having strutted across the empty square in front of his men, the centurion marched into the chief's house, followed by his optio and the soothsayer.

In the doorway, he made a big scene out of telling a legionary, 'You're to go to Rome, bearing a message for Caesar. You will tell him: "All Gaul is occupied." He will ask: "All?" You will reply: **"ALL."** He will understand.'

'As Caesar might say: "I came, I saw, I conquered." Well done, soothsayer! You know your job!'

The optio insisted on sending the soothsayer along too. After all, orders had come from Rome for all Gaulish soothsayers to be imprisoned, and now that this one's predictions had turned out true, they could afford to get rid of him.

The soothsayer protested. 'I'm not a real soothsayer! I'm only a con man.'

But carried away by his easy success, the centurion wanted more. He insisted on knowing what the gods said about his future. 'Answer me, or I'll have you opened up so you can read your own entrails!'

'But listen, I told them the air in the village would turn foul!' said the soothsayer, clinching his argument.

The centurion wrinkled up his nose, sniffing the air.

'I say, do you smell a funny kind of smell all of a sudden?'

And the three of them immersed themselves in a study of the atmosphere. Just then the door opened, letting in a pale-faced legionary.

'Centurion, the air in this village isn't fit to breathe!' he gasped. 'It's pestilential!'

Everyone rushed outside. A column of smoke was rising from the clearing. The whole village was enveloped in thick, sickly vapours. The Roman soldiers, overcome, had gone green and were lying about the place higgledy-piggledy, feeling sick. Romans have very sensitive noses.

No sooner had they arrived than they were off again. Orders were issued to evacuate the village.

It was only too obvious that Getafix still hadn't found a potion to cure him. He had simply concocted a mixture giving off such a stink that it put the Roman soldiers to flight, which of course was no bad thing.

Nor had our druid lost the habit of cackling with diabolical laughter which he'd had ever since that wretched menhir struck. He was high . . . high above the cloud of noxious vapours. A bubbling mixture spurted from the cauldron in its crater. Oops! Getafix opened his mouth and caught some in passing. The effect was startling. He spat fire, his eyes popped out of his head. His face swelled up and distorted. He roared – with pain, this time. Only then, in his crazed mind, did something go click. The explosive potion had cured him. He saw me lying there half-conscious on the rock, with Dogmatix watching over me. Anxiously, he called out to me.

The mists had slowly cleared from my own brain too. As I was sitting up, I heard the druid's voice.
'Asterix, can you hear me?'
'Getafix, you're cured!'
I rose and ran to his arms. At last our druid could put an end to the whole ridiculous business!

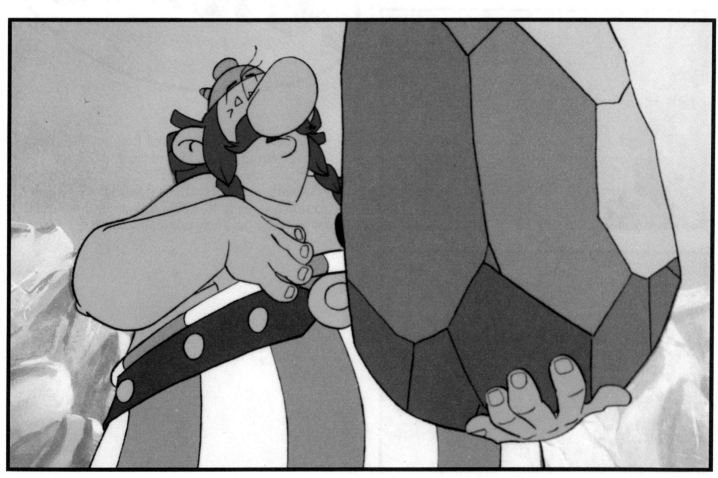

BOOOOM!!

Large as Obelix is, he can manage to slip off unnoticed. Seeing all Getafix's attempts at self-medication fail, he had gone into the forest, feeling gloomy.

'It's all my fault,' he told himself. 'To think that a little tap with a menhir . . . wait a minute! **A tap with a menhir!!!**

Perhaps another tap would rearrange Getafix's mind? Wasn't there a name for the method – curing something bad by something else bad? Anyway, what did he risk?

There was another **BOOOM!** The menhir landed right on Getafix. I was tearing my hair, red in the face with fury. It just couldn't be possible!

'Obelix! Did you throw that menhir?'

'Of course I did. To cure our druid. You're not going to tell me I've done the wrong thing yet again?' said Obelix, crossly.

What did I do to deserve a friend like that? The whole nightmare was beginning again. Then, suddenly we heard the druid's muffled voice.

'Stop arguing and get me out of here!' it said.

We carefully lifted the menhir off him.

'Toutatis be praised! Our druid is still cured!' I cried.

And Obelix, who is always a bit slow on the uptake, except with menhirs, said, **'What do you mean, still? I'VE just cured him with my careful treatment!'**

Oh, all right. No point in arguing.

Getafix suggested going to find the other villagers. We had to make sure the soothsayer was exposed. So we set off!

The centurion, pleased with himself, had gone back to camp with his legionaries. He could already feel the laurel wreath on his brow. One, the indomitable Gauls had been driven out of Armorica. Two, the soothsayer was a genuine soothsayer. He took him off to his tent.

'I could have you arrested,' he said, 'but you might yet come in useful. With your predictions and your advice I could go far. I could get to be **Caesar**.'

'You think I'm a soothsayer. A real soothsayer,' said the fraud. 'But I'm not!'

'You won't find me ungrateful.'

So saying, the centurion threw him a purse of gold coins. Faced with such a convincing argument, the soothsayer felt his doubts evaporate. He began to accept the idea. Perhaps he was a real soothsayer, after all.

He came down to earth with a thump. Getafix had just appeared in the opening of the tent. He stood there, hands on hips.

'Who are you, and what do you want?' gasped the soothsayer.

'Well, you win, soothsayer!' said the druid, smiling.

'I win? Win what?'

'Can't you foresee what?' said Getafix. And the Gaulish ladies, led by Impedimenta, entered the tent.

'Oh, didn't you foresee this?' she inquired.

She had come armed with her rolling pin, and now she showed what a talented cook she was. She floored the soothsayer with one well-aimed blow, and the centurion with another. Outside, her friends were letting off steam, attacking any legionary within rolling-pin range with every sign of satisfaction. They had gone right through the camp in no time.

Meanwhile, on the roads of Armorica, a Roman chariot was galloping along. It carried an envoy from Caesar, who arrived in the Roman camp just as the battle was raging. He had to stand by powerless and watch our victorious charge. Perched on a broken branch, he exchanged pleasantries with the centurion.

'Julius Caesar . . . told me to check up . . . and see if you'd really conquered the rebel Gauls.' Bulbus Crocus, Caesar's special envoy, wasn't mincing his words. **'And look what your conquered Gauls did to us, by Jupiter!'**

'It's not my fault!' protested the centurion. 'It was that fraud of a soothsayer who . . . .'

'Silence! You're reduced to the ranks!!!'

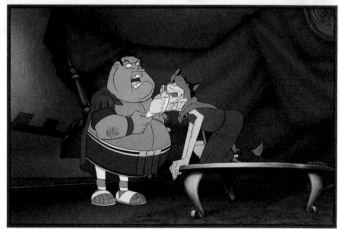

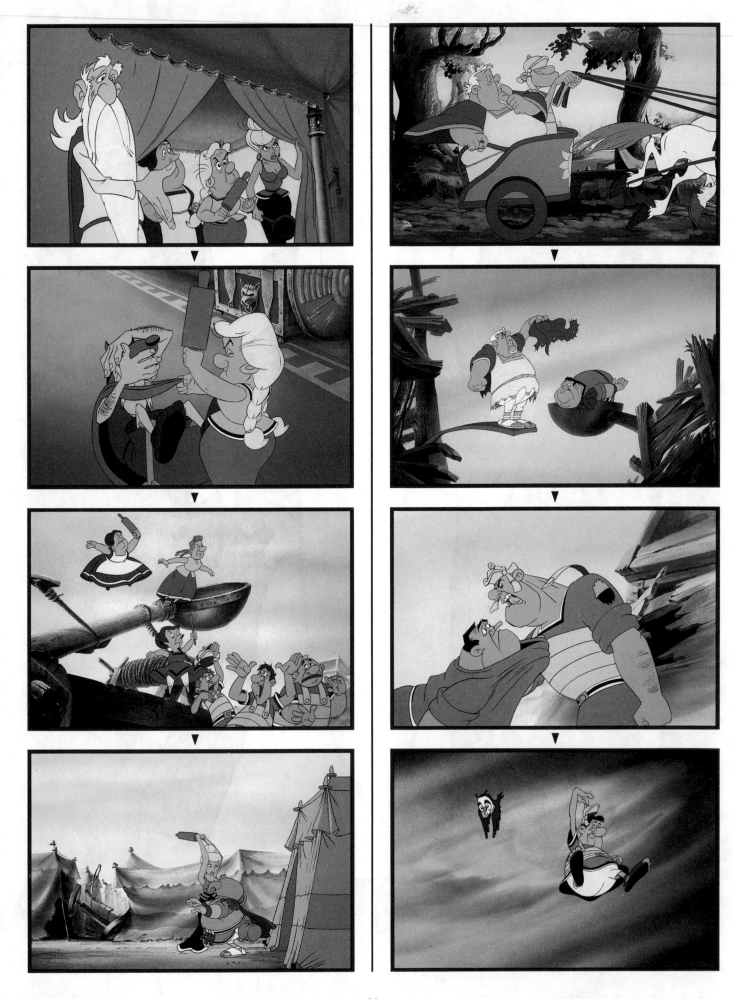

BOOOOM!

The battle was over. For once, the menfolk of the village had been on the sidelines. The ladies have a different but very efficacious technique. In the general confusion, no one was paying any attention to the soothsayer, who tried to slip away as discreetly as possible. No such luck. Dogmatix still had a bone to pick with him. He set off in pursuit, caught up, and clung to his caligae.

'There goes the dog reader!' yelled Obelix.

Without more ado, he sent a large menhir flying that way. **BOOOOOM!** You could see he'd been practising a lot lately. The menhir was a bull's-eye. The soothsayer emerged from under it, looking rather older, and curiously absent-minded.

'Ladies and gentlemen . . . hic!'

He was obviously a changed man. Can menhirs really have psychological effects after all?

'Come on, let's get back to the village,' I suggested.

We left a devastated camp behind us. But things were already changing. Spotting the soothsayer, the centurion made for him, calling the optio.

'Optio, arrest this impostor!'

'I don't take no orders from a common legionary!' said the optio. **'You can sweep out this camp on your own!'** And turning to the soothsayer, he said, 'Get out! No civilians allowed inside this camp!'

Taking advantage of the chaos, the flying legionary Infirmofpurpus undid the rope tethering him and spread his wings, imitated by his friend the owl.

That evening, the village was its usual cheeful self again. Under the starry sky of our beautiful Gaul, we were all re-united for a great banquet. Obelix's favourite food, roast boar, was on on the menu. And everyone was telling the tale of the events of the last few hours . . . everyone, with a single exception, once again, if we were going to enjoy our banquet in peace, we had to silence our hopelessly unmusical bard Cacofonix.

And high, high in the sky we saw the distant form of Infirmofpurpus, making for somewhere quieter . . .